# Giada De Laurentiis's
# *Recipe for Adventure*

## *Naples!*

written with Taylor Morris
illustrated by Francesca Gambatesa

Grosset & Dunlap
An Imprint of Penguin Group (USA)

GROSSET & DUNLAP
Published by the Penguin Group
Penguin Group (USA) Inc., 375 Hudson Street, New York, New York 10014, USA

USA | Canada | UK | Ireland | Australia | New Zealand | India | South Africa | China
Penguin Books Ltd, Registered Offices: 80 Strand, London WC2R 0RL, England

For more information about the Penguin Group visit penguin.com

Text copyright © 2013 by GDL Foods, Inc. Illustrations copyright © 2013 by Francesca Gambatesa.
Published by Grosset & Dunlap, a division of Penguin Young Readers Group, 345 Hudson Street, New York, New York 10014.
GROSSET & DUNLAP is a trademark of Penguin Group (USA) Inc. Printed in the U.S.A.

ISBN 978-0-448-46256-1 (pbk)                      10 9 8 7 6 5 4 3 2 1
ISBN 978-0-448-47853-1 (hc)                       10 9 8 7 6 5 4 3 2 1

ALWAYS LEARNING                                                    PEARSON

This book is dedicated to my aunt Raffy, who always inspires me to be adventurous in cooking and in life!

Questo libro è dedicato a mia zia Raffy, che ispira sempre che io sia avventurosa in cucina e nella vita!

# Chapter 1

"Alfredo!" Mom called from the kitchen as she flipped open two Presto Pesto pizza boxes in the middle of the table. "Let's go! Dinner! Emilia! You too!"

Alfie gladly tossed aside his geography homework—his favorite subject—and ran down the hall to the kitchen. He loved maps, but he loved food more. In the kitchen, he reached across the table and scooped up a slice of Supreme Meat Machine pizza, which sagged under the weight of three kinds of meat, four kinds of cheese, and two kinds of olives. Alfie tilted his head back, aimed the tip of the slice into his open mouth, and started backing out of the kitchen.

"Hang on," Mom said. "Where do you think you're going?"

"*Mmph rooph*. Learning about *rifers* in Egypt."

"You eat at the table with the *famiglia*. Sit down and get a napkin," Mom said. "Where's your sister?"

His sister, Emilia, older by just one year, entered the kitchen with her eyes glued to the history textbook in her hand. She looked up and inspected the pizza boxes.

"Why are we having pizza now?" she asked. "We're in charge of bringing pizza to school on Friday for United Nations Day." Their school was going to "taste the foods of the world," as

Emilia's teacher, Ms. Esch, said. Alfie and Emilia, whose classes would be combined for one afternoon, offered to bring pizza to represent the food of Italy, since that's where their family was from.

"Mauricio! *Andiamo! Mangiamo!*" Mom called to the kids' dad, as she slid a slice of pizza onto a paper plate.

"Then that'll be three times this week," Emilia said with a sigh as she stared at the pizza.

"That's why this week rules," Alfie said. Why did his sister love to act like awesome things weren't awesome?

Emilia inspected Alfie's spread. "You can't eat all the meat slices. Mom, he's taking all the Supreme Meat."

"I'm a growing man," Alfie said. "I need protein."

"Please, you're barely eleven," Emilia said. "Give me one, *boy*." She tried to snatch one off his plate, but he quickly pulled it away. "Mom! Tell *Alfredo* to give me the Supreme Meat." She used his proper name just to bug him—he despised his given name, which is why he went by the nickname Alfie.

"Kids, share," Mom said. "Emilia, pull your hair back. It's getting in your slice." She brushed Emilia's long, wavy hair, which was golden at the ends, back over her shoulder.

"I got it," Emilia said. She tucked her hair into the back of her fuchsia shirt.

"You should cut that mop," Alfie said. "You look like a mermaid."

"I'll take that as a compliment."

*"Ciao, ciao!"* a voice called from the front door. "Hello, hello!" Dad was finally home.

"We're in here!" Mom hollered back.

"And I," Dad said, his voice getting closer, "found a surprise on our doorstep."

In the doorway stood a slim, tiny woman in ridiculously high heels. Her salt-and-pepper hair was tied back in a loose braid, showing off the chunky gold and multicolored-stone necklace around her neck. She wore a graphic T-shirt under a dark blazer, slim jeans, and roughed-up tan leather boots. She was older than their mom, but somehow the clothes looked right on her.

*"Ciao, famiglia!"* she said, spreading her arms wide. *"Bambina!* Arianna!" she said to Mom.

"Zia!" Mom said, using the Italian word for aunt and dropping her slice on the table with a *thunk*. She sprang from her seat, and she and Zia wrapped each other up in a tight, twirling hug, laughing and screaming the whole time. "Zia! Zia! You're here! *Come sta?"*

*"Molto bene!"* Zia laughed. *"Molto bene!"*

"I thought you were coming *next* week," Mom said to Zia Donatella, holding her tight around her small waist.

"You knew Donatella was coming?" Dad asked from the doorway.

"I'm sorry. Didn't I tell you?" Mom said.

Dad eyed Mom while he set down the two large suitcases.

Great-aunt Donatella was from Italy—just like their mom and dad—but she lived all over the world, traveling from country to country searching for adventures. It'd been a while since they'd seen her, but Alfie loved her visits. She told stories of places he'd never even thought of visiting. Zia Donatella gave him his first world map when he was five, pointing to a spot in Egypt where she had just seen ancient pyramids. Since then, Alfie covered his walls with maps, memorizing capitals, rivers, mountains, and everything else he thought might be useful for his future job as a professional explorer.

"Kids, give your great-aunt Donatella a hug!" Mom said.

While Emilia hugged Zia tightly around her waist, Alfie stood at a cool distance. As excited as he was to see her, he was getting older and didn't think he should hug her like she was Santa Claus at the mall.

"My goodness, how you've both grown!" Zia Donatella said. When Emilia finally released Zia from her hug, Zia stepped closer to Alfie, taking his face in her hands. Alfie couldn't help but smile. *"Bello!"*

"Want some dinner?" Alfie offered. "We got pizza!"

Zia Donatella looked at the cardboard boxes and slices of pizza on the table, now cooled with sweating cheese on top. *"Ma che mangiate?* What are you eating? This is your dinner?"

"Don't start, Zia Donatella," Mom said, combining the remaining pizza into one box and tossing the other. "We're just busy. Besides, we're not amazing chefs like you are."

"It doesn't take a chef to cook a homemade meal, *ragazza*," Zia said.

"Zia, have you run into any bulls lately?" Alfie asked, remembering the story she had told of watching bulls race through a Spanish town; she was almost pummeled by them.

Zia Donatella smiled and said, "Thankfully, no. But I did see a wildebeest in Namibia."

"That's awesome!"

"He tasted pretty good, too," she said, winking.

Alfie was so stunned that for a moment he couldn't react. Then he said, "Mom! Can we have wildebeest for dinner tomorrow night?"

"I don't think the Save 'n Shop here carries that," Mom said.

Eyeing the pizza, Zia said, "Does this food you're eating have a name?"

"Fast," Emilia said, making Alfie snort out a laugh as she tried to hide her own giggle.

"Zia, don't you know pizza when you see it?" Alfie asked because—seriously!—it was food from their motherland!

"You poor children. You really think this is pizza." Zia looked more upset than offended. "Let me cook something," Zia said, pushing back her chair. "*Mi piace molto cuocere!* I love to cook!"

"Zia," Mom said, but Zia had already started digging

through the pantry. She found canned fruit cocktail, individually wrapped cinnamon rolls, and boxed mac and cheese. She held a can of peas up to Mom and asked, "Will I find anything fresh in the refrigerator?"

"Why don't we get you settled in?" Dad suggested. "Tomorrow we can shop. Honey?" he said to Mom, asking with a nod where to put Zia's bags.

"Well, why don't you take . . . ?" She looked between Emilia and Alfie. They knew what was coming—someone was about to lose his or her room.

Emilia sat up straight in a desperate attempt to show how responsible she was and therefore how deserving of keeping her room. Alfie tried the opposite approach. He murdered the last slice of Supreme Meat Machine, hoping to show Mom how messy he was and that no one in her right mind would ever put any human in his room. It was strictly an "at your own risk" sort of place.

"You can take . . . Alfie's room," Mom declared.

"Mom!" Alfie said. "That's not fair!"

"Emilia is the oldest," Mom said.

"But I'm the man!" he said.

"Ha! You wish," Emilia said.

Alfie felt bad about being rude in front of Zia Donatella, but he couldn't believe he was getting kicked out of his room. "Where am I going to sleep?"

"Well," Mom said, thinking. "Maybe you could bunk in Emilia's room?"

"No!" he and Emilia both yelled at the same time. At least they agreed on that.

"He can take the pullout sofa in the office," Dad said. "If we put an air mattress on top, it's not that bad."

*"Not that bad,"* Alfie thought. *Translation: future spine surgery may be required.*

"Great, then it's settled," Mom said. "But first, Alfredo, get that room straightened up."

Alfie sulked to his room to clean it up—and to say *arrivederci* to his privacy.

## Chapter 2

Sleep was impossible in the so-called bed. It was more like sleeping on a bag full of baseballs. Alfie's parents hadn't been able to find the pump for the air mattress, so Dad said he'd have to tough it out for the night. Noises from the kitchen also kept him awake.

It was probably Zia Donatella, who loved creating new dishes inspired by her travels. Her arrival had been so chaotic, she hadn't had time to tell them any new stories.

A loud bang came from the kitchen, and since Alfie couldn't sleep anyway, he decided to get up to inspect. He ran into Emilia in the hall.

"Can't sleep, either?" he whispered.

"Nah," she said.

They heard another clang in the kitchen.

"Guess Zia can't, either," Alfie said.

Emilia nodded. "Let's go see what she's up to."

They headed down the darkened hall together. When they entered the kitchen, Alfie smiled at the scene created by Zia Donatella. Every light was on and the contents of the cabinets were scattered across the countertops—bags of flour and sugar, spices, bowls, spoons, and more. In the middle of all of it was Zia Donatella, dressed in a long, flowing gown, black and red with bits of gold. Alfie couldn't tell if it was a dress or a nightgown, but what did it matter—it had a huge dragon snaking around from the back to the front, which made it the greatest whatever-it-was he'd ever seen.

"Zia," Alfie said in a loud whisper. He didn't want his parents to wake up, although with all this noise, it was a miracle they hadn't already.

Zia Donatella turned from the refrigerator with a

carton of eggs in her hand. "Hello, my *bambini*," she said.

"I was wondering when you were going to visit me."

Alfie and Emilia leaned on the counter. Alfie's forearms were immediately coated in flour. "What are you doing?" he asked as he dusted off the flour.

"It's a miracle you have any actual food in here," she said, inspecting her ingredients. "But when you're clever, you can always find something to cook up. So—I cook."

"In the middle of the night?" Emilia asked.

Zia Donatella stopped for a moment, resting her hand on her hip. "I'm homesick," she said. "Have you ever been homesick?"

"It's hard to get homesick when you hardly ever go anywhere," Alfie said. "Our last vacation was three summers ago."

"Mom and Dad just get busy with work," Emilia said, defending their parents. "But they promise we'll go somewhere next summer."

"Or the one after that," Alfie said, nudging his sister and making her smile.

"Well, I hope someday you know the feeling," Zia

said. "It's always good to get away and see the world, but there's nothing like feeling connected to your home and feeling the need to go back, even for a visit."

"But you're here now," Emilia said. "Don't you feel better?"

"Not this home!" Zia said, waving her away. "My home. Your parents' home. Your *nonna*'s home."

"You mean Naples, in Italy," Alfie said.

*"Esatto,"* Zia said. "Exactly." She stepped back to the stove, where she heated oil in a deep skillet. "Once, I was in the Philippines and we discovered a place called Boracay with the most beautiful beaches I'd ever seen in my life. Clear water and sand as white as sugar. But suddenly, despite the beauty of the place, I felt this ache in my heart for home. Home to me meant plates of spaghetti, bowls of risotto, and fresh fish straight from the sea. I realized that if I found the right ingredients, I could cook the things I missed. And so I made my new friends the most amazing fish with lemon and spaghetti." Zia tossed

a dash of salt into the mixing bowl in front of her, then paused as if thinking fondly of the dish. "The spaghetti may have been a little more Filipino than Italian, but the feeling was still there. I tasted home in my cooking. When you cook from the heart you can go anywhere in the world without getting on a plane. Much less expensive," she said with a wink. She added flour and a few other ingredients to the bowl. "Besides, I couldn't sleep thinking about that wretched pizza you poor children were eating. Pizza—how dare you even call it that!"

"Come on, Zia," Alfie said. He had to admit it was kind of fun to see her get so riled up over the pizza. "I thought you'd be happy about us eating food from Italy."

"That's not food!" she snapped as she added butter to the bowl and turned on the mixer. "And it's certainly not Italian."

"Look, Zia," Alfie said over the noise of the mixer. "Italian food is in my genes. And Presto Pesto is good Italian food."

"Good Italian—oh my goodness, you kids," Zia said. Emilia giggled, but she also nudged Alfie to tell him to go easy on the teasing.

Zia turned off the mixer and removed the attachment. "When I was a little girl in Naples, I ate the best pizza every week and didn't even realize it. Nowhere else in the world can make pizza that good."

"What's so special about it?" Emilia asked.

"Oh, nothing much," Zia said. "Just the dough and the sauce and the cheese and the basil. Not to mention the way the dough is made, how the tomatoes and basil are grown, the hands used to stretch the cheese . . ."

"Hands that make cheese?" Alfie said. "I'd like to see that."

"You will, I assure you. They'll show you themselves," Zia said.

"Who will?" Alfie asked.

"*I* will show you myself," Zia said. "Do you know what else is wonderful about Naples? Emilia, can you please hand me that slotted spoon."

Emilia handed her the spoon and asked, "What, Zia?"

Zia took her mixture to the pan of hot oil on the stove, scooped up balls of dough, and dropped them into the hot oil. "The chaos!" she said, stepping back from the sizzling pops and crackles of oil. "Naples is full of contradictions—beautiful cathedrals on streets with dark alleys. It's loud, it's fast, it's a little dirty in some places. But the people are wonderful and the food is always fresh—even the street food. Like the zeppole." She scooped out some of the fried balls and rested them on a plate covered with a paper towel.

"Is that what these are?" Emilia asked, leaning over the plate.

"*Sí*," she said. "When I was a little girl, my sister—your *nonna*, your grandmother—and I would walk the winding streets together, never once getting lost. Any money we had in our pockets we'd always use to buy zeppole from a street vendor. We'd walk down to the park and eat them as we looked out at the water."

"That's the Gulf of Naples, right?" Alfie said, trying to picture Italy on his maps.

"*Perfetto!* The Gulf of Naples that flows to the Mediterranean Sea," Zia said. "Water like you've never seen. You're going to love it. But for now—the zeppole." She moved the plate closer to Alfie and Emilia, then brought over another. "Sugar and cinnamon," she said, pointing to the second plate. She took a small spice jar from the counter and dipped a teaspoon into it. "Now Alfie, since you so gallantly gave up your room, you must add the magical ingredient—nutmeg."

Alfie sprinkled the nutmeg over the cinnamon-and-sugar-filled plate. He glanced at the jar, noticing that it didn't look like the other spice jars they had—but then again, when had he ever really paid attention?

With the nutmeg added, Zia cheered, "*Perfetto!* Now quickly, *bambini*—roll them around in the mixture while they're still warm."

Alfie and Emilia picked up a warm zeppole each and

rolled it around in the mixture, coating it on all sides.

"*Aspetta*. Wait before you taste," Zia Donatella said. "I want you to picture the narrow cobblestoned streets. Voices rising all around you. Walking past stands of fresh fruit and restaurants with tables spilling out onto the sidewalks, the sounds and the smells wrapping around you. Now," she said, leaning in close, "taste that zeppole and tell me you don't feel the city around you."

Alfie and Emilia did as they were told, sinking their teeth into the warm fried dough, crunchy on the outside and soft on the inside. Little crystals of sugar coated Alfie's lips. He closed his eyes as he chewed the light, sweet zeppole, wondering if his parents were ever going to take him and his sister to Italy. He wanted to know what it felt like to walk on cobblestones, to feel the fresh sea air on his face . . .

# Chapter 3

And breathe in the smell of pizza made from scratch.
Alfie started to take another bite when he felt the air shift
slightly around him.

*"Ragazzo! Vieni qui!"*

A man standing behind a cart was yelling at him.
When Alfie looked more closely, he saw that he was
selling zeppole—just like Zia Donatella had made.

Looking around, it was clear he was not in his parents'
kitchen with his sister and Zia. He was standing on a
street so narrow that the sun couldn't reach it through the
stone buildings. The street and sidewalk were crowded
with people, and cars and scooters were zipping by.

"I said come here! You take, you pay double. You and the girl," he said.

Alfie turned to see that his sister standing beside him, rigid. Her blue eyes were wider and more frightened than he'd ever seen them, even that time he jumped out of her closet to scare her.

"Al-Alfie . . . ," she said. "What's happening . . . ?"

"It's okay," he said automatically, even though he had no idea where they were or what had happened. Two chatting girls brushed past them. Emilia moved closer to Alfie.

The man behind the cart started to approach them. He wore a striped apron, and the little paper hat on his head sat at an irritated angle. Alfie quickly reached into his jeans' pockets and thankfully found a dollar. He stepped toward the man and handed it to him. "Here. I'm sorry."

The man snatched the bill from Alfie's hand, frightening him. Alfie had never been yelled at by an adult

before, but since he could feel his sister shaking beside him, he knew he had to be brave.

The man looked at the dollar and started yelling a

whole new string of questions. "What is this? Where do you think you are? Disney World? I don't want your American money!"

"That's all I have," Alfie said, trying to sound calm.

"You want me to call the police or you want to pay up, boy?" He shoved the dollar back at Alfie. "You have three seconds."

"Alfie," Emilia said, her voice coming in short breaths. "What are we going to do?"

"Hey! Officer!" the man yelled to someone across the street.

"Alfie . . . ," Emilia said, and Alfie knew she was on the verge of crying.

"We got a thief over here!"

Alfie reached down and grabbed Emilia's hand. He tugged it and said, "Run!"

Alfie and Emilia took off down the tight, winding streets, splashing in puddles and bumping into people who turned to yell at them. They hid around a corner. Alfie looked back and was just able to see that the man had stopped chasing them. Relieved, Alfie led his sister to where the streets widened and the sun shone down on them. They slowed to a walk, and Alfie let go of Emilia's hand.

"What is going on?" Emilia asked. "Where are we? What is this place? Why was that guy yelling at us?"

"I don't know," Alfie said, trying to catch his breath. He had to think rationally. "I must be dreaming. I'm having a dream and you're in it."

"I'm not in your dream," Emilia said. "You're in my dream. Get out of my dream!" She reached over and pinched him several times before he could yank his arm away.

"Emilia, stop it," Alfie said. "We can't both be dreaming the same dream at the same time." He looked down at his left hand, which still clutched the zeppole. Sugar, cinnamon, and nutmeg stuck to his palm. "The zeppole!"

Emilia looked at the zeppole in her own hand. She screamed and threw it across the street, hitting a woman wearing a red-and-white-striped skirt. The woman yelled something back to Emilia that she didn't understand. Emilia stepped closer to her brother once again. "The guy must think we stole them!"

"Nice move," Alfie said, gently teasing her.

"Be quiet," she said. She crossed her arms and looked around. "Well, you like to pretend you're a grown-up and in charge, so here's your chance—what are we going to do?"

Alfie surveyed his surroundings. "Maybe there's something down this street here."

"If we keep walking around, we'll get lost."

"We're already lost," Alfie reminded her. "We have no idea where we are or how we got here."

Emilia looked back the way they had come. "Maybe being by that cart means something. Should we go back?"

"I'm pretty sure we shouldn't go anywhere near that cart ever again," Alfie said. "Just let me think for a minute." He had to make sure he didn't panic because, after all, this probably was some sort of weird dream—which meant it wasn't even real. But dream or no dream, he had to take care of his sister, even though she was starting to look less frightened and more annoyed.

Alfie looked around. He spotted the word *Napoli* on a shop window and on a stack of newspapers. Tiny cars rushed by them, half the size of the cars he was used to seeing. People on scooters buzzed by without regard for others crossing the street—streets that were cobblestoned, with rivers of water running between the stones. He looked up to the corner to find the street names—they were on the corner of Via Salvator Rosa and Via Pontecorvo. On the wall of a brick building, faded white letters read PASTA FABBRICA. He made a note of this, marking it as a point of reference of where this whole thing started. Up ahead was a restaurant called Trattoria Floreano with tables set up outside. Alfie was pretty sure that all these words were Italian.

"Didn't the guy selling zeppole say something about being in Disney World?" he asked his sister. "Maybe we're at Epcot in the Italian section!"

"Yeah, sure," Emilia said. "Because that makes sense."

"I keep seeing the word *Napoli*. That's *Naples* in Italian, right?"

"Yeah, so?" Emilia said. "What does it *mean*?"

"Maybe we're in Naples, Italy," he said.

"Alfie," Emilia began. "That doesn't make any sense."

Alfie sighed. She was right. "Let's go to that café and figure out what to do. If we stand here much longer, we'll get run over. Do you have any money on you?"

"Guess I forgot to grab my wallet before we left," she said sarcastically.

*We're not really in Italy*, he said to himself. But where

were they? They'd go to the café, order a Coke, and try to figure out what to do. "Come on. I'll take care of this."

Alfie walked behind Emilia as they headed toward Trattoria Floreano. With the streets so crowded and chaotic, the last thing he wanted was to lose sight of her. To their right, rising higher than all the buildings, he saw a white-peaked mountain, the top touching the clouds. "That's pretty cool looking, right?" he asked his sister, hoping to distract her.

"You know what's in Naples, Italy?" Emilia asked. "Mount Vesuvius."

"Okay . . . ," Alfie said.

"You know, the volcano that destroyed the entire city of Pompeii? The volcano that hasn't erupted in so many years that it's due for another blow?"

Alfie looked up at the mountain. It was bold and intimidating.

"I'm sure it'll be fine," he said. "I mean, what are the odds?"

# Chapter 4

"We're so going to get arrested," Emilia said, eyeing the small restaurant. "That dollar isn't going to buy us anything but a trip to jail."

"Let's just try," Alfie said. There were several small round tables outside on the narrow patio where couples were drinking coffees with frothy tops and eating pizzas that looked nothing like the ones from Presto Pesto. The pizzas were thin and hardly had any toppings.

"I'll go in just for the smell," Emilia said, taking a deep breath. His sister was right—a rich, sweet scent drifted over the smell of Vespa exhaust.

Alfie led the way into the restaurant, trying to find a

face that looked helpful and friendly. But everyone who worked here looked busy and stressed.

"It's busy in here," he said.

"Great observation," Emilia said.

He was about to tell her to stop being snippy when he tripped over something—some*one*.

"Watch it!" a voice said as Alfie stumbled, catching himself just before crashing into a table full of drinks and pizza.

Alfie looked down at the person sprawled on the floor and said, "I'm so sorry. Are you okay?"

"I'm okay." The person stood up; it was a boy about Alfie's age with dark, curly hair. He picked his tray up from the floor and dusted off his apron. "Luckily I'd already delivered the cappuccinos. The last thing I need on a day like today is for anything to go wrong."

"Tell me about it," Alfie said. "You sure you're okay? I'm really sorry."

"Yes, yes, I'm fine," the boy said. He gave a heavy sigh and began to walk away.

"Wait," Alfie called. He couldn't let him get away—not when the alternative was to go talk to one of the frantic adults behind the counter. Alfie watched as one man slid a pizza into a brick-domed oven while another man slid one out. It looked nothing like the Supreme Meat Machine. These pizzas only had red sauce and white discs of cheese. Snore.

"You can take any available table," the boy said over his shoulder as he went to the counter to pick up several glass bottles of Coke, which he deposited on his tray.

"Actually, I have a question," Alfie said. He heard Emilia mutter, "*One* question?" He ignored her and asked the most important thing: "Where are we?"

The boy hustled across the restaurant to deliver the drinks; Alfie followed him. "Via Salvator Rosa."

"Yeah but I mean . . . ," Alfie began, knowing he sounded crazy. He felt crazy. "Where *exactly*?"

The boy eyed Alfie. "Tourists, huh? Well, this is officially the Materdei area of town. If you're looking for the archaeology museum, it's just a couple of streets over. I can give you directions in a minute if you want." He dropped off the drinks and then set his tray down on a counter.

"I just—wait," Alfie said, feeling desperate.

"Papà! I'm going now!" the boy called to one of the men in the back as he took off his apron. A man with dark hair and olive skin—and a tomato-sauce-stained apron— waved good-bye to him. "I must go to the market. You're staying for tonight's *Festa di Pizza*, right?"

"Tonight's *Festa . . .*?"

"I must go to the market. If you want to ask more questions, you'll have to come with me."

"Uh, yeah," Alfie said. "We were going to check out the market, too."

Alfie looked back at Emilia, who shrugged. As the boy started out the door, Alfie said to his sister, "Let's try this."

"Alfie," Emilia said, grabbing his arm, "I think we

should stay here. Ask an adult."

Alfie looked around. It was chaos behind the brick counter; adults were cooking pizzas and taking food orders. Out in the restaurant, customers ate pizza, and one couple acted all kissy-kissy. That was definitely something Alfie could do without seeing.

"This guy is already talking to us," Alfie said. "I don't want to start over."

Her eyes followed the boy out the door. They had to act fast. "Fine. But for the record, I think we should stay."

"Stay and do what?" Alfie asked. He knew she didn't have any better ideas.

Back out in the street, the boy said, "Ready?" They nodded. "Today of all days is not the one to slow down anyone in my family. Anyone in all of Naples who is making pizza, for that matter. *Andiamo!*"

"Naples!" Emilia said, her eyes widening.

"As in Florida?" Alfie asked.

"Florida?" the boy said. "You're joking. You must be,

because this is the true Naples—Italy, the best city in all the world. Just look!"

Alfie recognized the street they turned on as one they had passed on their escape from the zeppole vendor. Old women wore scarves over their hair, and teenage girls—whom Emilia eyed enviously as they walked so confidently—wore cut-off shorts and stacked bracelets.

"To me," the boy continued, "this is very special, but of course I'm biased since I'm born and raised here. But Naples has everything you want, even the grit, if that's what you like. We're tough but fair. And our pizza—it's also the best in all the world!"

Alfie smiled at Emilia. He liked this guy, and his enthusiasm was infectious. Emilia giggled, covering her mouth.

They turned up a street narrower than the one they'd just left. "Did you come here just for it?" the boy asked.

"For what?" Alfie asked.

"*Festa di Pizza*, of course! And my family is the best

*pizzaioli* in all of Naples. Our Neapolitan pizza can't be beat—unless, of course, someone else decides to cheat and steal the title from us," he added bitterly. Alfie noticed he clenched his fists by his sides. "But not this year. This year we take back what is rightfully ours. Oh, hello, Signora Manichelli!" He waved to an elderly woman across the street. "That's Signora Manichelli. She feeds all the stray cats in the neighborhood. So. How long are you in town for?" They turned down another zigzagging street. Alfie tried his best to remember each twist and turn so that he could find his way back to the restaurant. When neither Alfie nor Emilia answered— how could they?—the boy said, "You are tourists, right?"

"Yes," Emilia said. "We're here on vacation."

"With your parents?" he asked.

"Yes," Alfie said, thinking quickly. He remembered Zia Donatella telling them just moments ago—what *seemed* like moments ago—about the Gulf of Naples and the cool breeze off the water. Alfie realized he could feel a salty breeze every now and then despite the tight turns of the streets. "But they're not here today. They're—they're down at the coast. Taking a boat ride."

"At La Grotta Azzurra?" he asked.

"Um, yes. What you said," Alfie said.

The boy pulled a list from his pocket. "I have to go now as well," he said. "I'm in charge of gathering all the ingredients for the pizza festival tonight."

"Maybe we could help you," Alfie heard Emilia say. He turned to her, ready to tell her to be quiet, but she shrugged and said, "We don't have anything else to do." He supposed she was right.

"That would be great," the boy said. "I can show you the best of Naples, and then you can taste the best pizza ever created in all of pizza history!"

Alfie looked to Emilia and the boy. Emilia seemed to feel confident about this adventure, even excited. He could see it in the little twinkle she had in her eyes. Maybe his sister was right—since they didn't know what else to do, they might as well just go along for the ride.

"Yeah, sure," Alfie said, and Emilia grinned. "We'll help."

"Great!" he said. "I'm Marco Floreano, by the way."

"Alfie Bertolizzi, and this is my sister, Emilia."

"Alfie as in Alfredo?" Marco asked, and Alfie braced himself for the stupid sauce jokes that always followed. He nodded yes and Marco said, "I have an uncle named Alfredo, so it'll be easy for me to remember. Well, Alfredo and Emilia, it's very nice to meet you both."

"Nice to meet you, too," Emilia said, and she shook Marco's hand, doing her best to be polite and act grown-up.

"Welcome to Naples," Marco said. "Get ready for the most exciting day of your lives!"

## Chapter 5

"This is the first year I'm in charge of gathering the ingredients," Marco said as he led the way through the crowded streets. They passed more people, some rushing along and dodging through pedestrian traffic and others strolling arm in arm. "First we go to the market to get the basil."

"What is the *Festa* ... uh, the pizza thing you were talking about?" Alfie asked. "Is it some sort of contest?"

"Only the most important contest in all of Naples. And it happens tonight," Marco said. "Every year the city has a contest to see who can make the best pizza in the place known for the world's best pizza. My family has won this honor for years—no one can beat our pizza. Until last year," Marco said bitterly, and Alfie noticed his fists clenching again.

"What happened last year?" Emilia asked.

"It was stolen from us," Marco said. "The so-called winners cheated."

Alfie and Emilia exchanged looks. Alfie wondered if there was some truth in what Marco said, or if he was being a sore loser. He wasn't about to ask, though.

"But this year," Marco continued, his mood lightening, "I'm in charge of gathering the ingredients. Since I'm twelve now, Papà says I'm ready."

"That's how old I am, too," Emilia said. She looked to Alfie and said, "I guess that makes you the baby."

Alfie wished she wouldn't tease him about being younger. He certainly didn't feel like he was the youngest.

"Emilia, watch your step," he said, guiding her away from a murky puddle that she wasn't even close to walking through. She smiled and stuck out her tongue at him. "Real mature," he muttered.

"So, Marco," Emilia said. "How many ingredients do we have to get?"

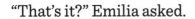

"Only a few," he said. "Basil, tomatoes, and mozzarella."

"That's it?" Emilia asked.

Alfie said, "The pizzas we eat usually have at least three toppings, not including sauce and cheese."

"If there are so many toppings, how do you taste the pizza?" Marco asked. This made absolutely no sense to Alfie. The toppings were what made the pizza, of course! "Papà always says that simple, fresh ingredients are what make all Italian foods so delicious. And first, the basil."

As they followed him, Emilia said to her brother, "Isn't it funny how Zia Donatella was just telling us about good pizza and Naples?"

"Funny or totally strange?" he said.

"What's that?" Marco asked.

"Nothing," Alfie said. "Hey, why not just go to the grocery store to get all the ingredients? Wouldn't it be faster and easier?"

Marco looked horrified. "We'd never! Signora Ricci sells us our basil."

They turned down Via Vecchia. The sides of the streets were lined with tables selling a colorful variety of everything imaginable, from herbs and spices to fresh fish and even ladies' handbags and sunglasses. People walked in the middle of the street despite the cars rolling along. Alfie steered Emilia to the side and kept an eye out for vans driving through to drop off goods at the tables. The last thing they needed was to get run over.

"Papà inspects every ingredient to make sure it's perfect," Marco told them. "Even the flour and olive oil.

And everything comes from right here in Naples. We buy basil from Signora Ricci here at the Mercato Pignasecca."

They followed him to a table that sat between a young girl selling olives and a couple selling leather sandals. Marco greeted the woman, who had a sturdy build despite being barely taller than Alfie. Signora Ricci gestured to the bunch of small green stems, and Marco began sniffing and eyeing each bunch.

"Smell," he said, holding a handful out to Emilia. As she took in a deep breath, Alfie noticed Marco look over his shoulder. Alfie followed his gaze and saw a boy, maybe about their age—tall and wiry with unruly hair— and wondered if that was who made Marco's eyes dark for a moment.

"So sweet and fragrant," Emilia said. "Like a flower you can eat."

"That's right," Marco said, turning back to Emilia and obviously pleased with her response. "These are the ones," he told Signora Ricci.

"Excellent choice, young man," she said. She wrapped them in a paper towel, then laid them in a plastic bag. Nodding down a couple of tables, she said, "Giuseppe has some amazing *mozzarella di bufala* today. Wait until you taste it. Guaranteed you'll get that title back."

Marco paid Signora Ricci and took the bag. "Thank you. But there's a special batch waiting for me up at the farm. That's where we're going now."

"Good luck, then," she said. "I know you'll get them this year!"

"Good-bye, Signora!" Marco waved and led them back out of the market. "So," he said, "I hope you don't mind going out of town a bit, because the next stop is just up the hill. A quick bus ride and we're there."

Alfie was beginning to enjoy this strange adventure, and since he knew cheese was one of Emilia's favorite things, he said, "Show us the way."

# Chapter 6

They all climbed aboard a bus, which Marco said would take them to the hills above town where they would find their next ingredient. Marco paid their bus fare. "It's the least I could do, since you're helping me," he said.

Alfie noticed Marco looking over his shoulder once again.

They walked down the aisle to take their seats. Alfie looked out the back and saw the boy from the market racing to catch the bus.

"Look," he said. "I think I saw him at the market. Do you know him?"

Marco scowled and sat in a seat. Emilia sat in front

of him by the window, and Alfie sat next to her. "Yes, unfortunately," Marco said. "That's Enzo. His family owns a restaurant that they think is better than ours. What a joke. They're the ones who beat us last year in the *Festa di Pizza*, but we think it's because they spied on us and learned where we got our ingredients. That's why we're making this special trip to the farm."

"But if you used the same ingredients from the same places, wouldn't the pizzas taste exactly the same?" Emilia asked.

"Every pizza is different," Marco said. "My *nonna* used to always say it's how you feel when you make it that matters, too. And last year, Papà spotted Enzo buying his mozzarella from Giuseppe at the market and that's how he knew they were just following us around. He was so angry when he made the pizza that the judges said the crust was too tough. What an insult," he said. "This year, you'll taste how light our dough is, crispy on the outside and soft on the inside. Total perfection made without a care in the world."

The bus stopped suddenly and they all watched as Enzo himself boarded the bus, panting from running.

"Oh, great," Marco muttered as Enzo passed them and found a seat a few rows back. As the bus moved again, Marco turned to him and said, "Can't you find the markets on your own?"

Enzo shrugged like it was no big deal. "It's a free country. I can take the bus anywhere I want."

Marco turned back around. "Incredible," he said, shaking his head. "Enzo will do anything to get what he wants. He just uses people."

"What a jerk," Alfie said. Alfie didn't get involved in his parents' business and could hardly imagine caring so much about it that he'd want to hurt another family.

Emilia looked back at Enzo, who pretended to gaze casually out the window but kept shooting glances in their direction.

"Are you crazy?" her brother said. He already felt a sense of allegiance to Marco. After all, he had selflessly helped them today, no questions asked. "He looks shady."

"I promise, he is," Marco said. "We'll have to ditch him at the next stop, okay?"

"You got it," Alfie said.

"When I say run, I mean run," Marco said to Alfie and Emilia. "Run."

"We got it," Alfie said, but Marco was getting up.

"No, I mean *run!*"

Alfie had been so busy shooting dirty looks to Enzo that he hadn't noticed the bus slow down for the next stop. The doors were about to close, and Marco was already halfway out. Alfie scrambled up and followed him, making it out just before the doors closed. Close call!

"Thank goodness," Marco said as the bus pulled away. "We lost him."

Alfie never knew something as simple as making pizza could become such an adventure—not to mention so cutthroat. But, he guessed, if you were going to be competitive about a particular food, pizza might as well be the one. It was, after all, the best food in the whole world.

"Come on," Marco said, turning on the gravel road. "We can walk the rest of the way. It's not far."

It wasn't until Alfie turned to make sure Emilia was okay with walking that he realized something that he probably should have noticed before the bus pulled away.

"Emilia?" he said, his voice on the verge of cracking.

Alfie watched helplessly as the bus drove off in a cloud of dust. Emilia was still on the bus—and getting farther and farther away from him.

# Chapter 7

"Emilia!" Alfie yelled as he frantically ran after the bus, pumping his arms and moving his legs as fast as they would go. It didn't take long to see that it was useless. He'd never catch up. His sister was gone forever.

Marco caught up with Alfie, and they both stood on the side of the road, trying to catch their breaths.

"What am I going to do?" Alfie said, panting. His heart raced, and not just from the sprint. "My sister—she's gone!"

Alfie couldn't believe this was happening. He thought he'd been good about keeping Emilia close, but it wasn't good enough. She must be so scared, alone on a bus in a foreign country. And they didn't even know *how* they were here in the first place. If he ever got her back, Alfie was sure Emilia was going to kill him for this.

"Marco, what are we going to do?" Alfie said, grabbing Marco by the shirt and practically shaking him.

"Okay, we'll figure it out, friend," Marco said. He put his hand on Alfie's shoulder.

"We gotta go get her," Alfie said. "We gotta find her." Alfie couldn't think beyond this thought, he was so scared for his sister. What if something happened to her? He'd never forgive himself.

"Maybe she got off at the next stop, hoping we'd meet her there," Marco said. "Let's run there and see."

It seemed like a logical plan, even in Alfie's frantic mind. Marco led the way, the two boys running down the road faster than Alfie had ever run in gym class, until they got to the next bus stop. Emilia wasn't there.

Both boys were panting, and Marco leaned on his knees to catch his breath.

"One more stop?" Alfie said, and Marco nodded. They took off again, running farther and faster than Alfie had ever run in his life. Emilia might be older and might think she was wiser, but Alfie knew his sister must be scared. He hated to think of her feeling like he left her, like he wasn't taking care of her.

At the next stop they found the same thing—nothing. Alfie was on the verge of panicking, but he knew he had to try his best to stay calm and come up with a plan.

"Maybe she got on a bus going back to town?" Alfie said, but he didn't believe it. They hadn't seen a bus going the other way. "Maybe she's going back to the restaurant, since that's where we started."

"Do you think she could find it again?" Marco asked.

"No," Alfie said. He'd worked hard to pay attention to where they went as they followed Marco to the market, but Alfie knew Emilia had just been taking in the sights. She'd never find the restaurant again. Still—where else might she be going? "But maybe I should go back down there anyway, just in case she finds her way."

"The bus back to town doesn't come for a little while longer," Marco said.

"Then I'll run down," Alfie said. "I know the way."

"How about this," Marco said. "Let's go to the mozzarella farm, and we'll use their phone to call the restaurant. We'll see if she's there and tell them to look out for her, just in case."

Alfie considered Marco's plan. Even though he didn't like the idea of getting farther away from his sister, he knew it was a better idea than trying to run all the way to town, which would take longer than going to make the phone call. "Okay," he said. "But as soon as we call and get the cheese, we're going straight back to Naples. Agreed?"

"Yes, of course," Marco said.

They walked up the hill, passed scraggly bushes and small farms selling olives, herbs, and other Italian goodies. When they got to the farm, Marco was warmly greeted by a slim and sun-browned young man who shook his hand and patted his back.

"Marco! Great to see you!" he said.

"Hello, Vito," Marco said. "How are things?"

"Great, great," Vito said. "Been busy. We've got lots of great—"

"Excuse me, can I use your phone, please?" Alfie said. He knew he was being rude, but at that moment he didn't care. He didn't care about cheese or being polite. He only cared about Emilia.

"This is my friend Alfredo," Marco said. "He's helping me with the ingredients, but we are having a bit of an emergency. Okay if we use your phone?"

"Sure, of course," Vito said, leading them into a squat wooden building that turned out to be the office. "Help yourself."

Alfie snatched the phone off the receiver, but he quickly realized he didn't know the restaurant's phone number or even how to dial it. Maybe phone numbers were different here in Italy?

He held the phone out to Marco and said, "I guess you should call."

"Thanks," Marco said.

The call to the restaurant was brief. When Marco hung up he said, "No sign of her." Alfie's stomach dropped. "I told them to keep an eye out for her and they promised they would. I know it's hard," Marco said, "but try not to worry. I'm sure she's okay. We'll find her."

"I hope you're right," Alfie said glumly. "Let's just get the cheese and get back to town."

Vito led them into a larger section of the farm. "I'm so glad to hear about you and your father's family," he said.

"What do you mean?" Marco asked.

"Enzo was here," Vito said, and Alfie was pretty sure that his and Marco's hearts both stopped beating. "He said he was buying for his restaurant and yours. He told me to play some game of not selling to you, but I don't have time for that."

"He was here?" Marco asked.

"Sure," Vito said. "You just missed him. Him and some girl. Said she was his cousin from out of town, which I guess is why she was a bit nervous. He said she'd never left her village before."

"Did he say where they were going next?" Alfie asked. His poor sister, being held as a hostage by Enzo!

"Back to the restaurant, I guess," Vito said. "They were trying to catch the next bus down."

"Let's go," Alfie said, turning to run out the door.

"Wait," Marco said. "I'm sorry, let's just get the cheese very fast. I must."

"But my sister," Alfie said.

"Two seconds, and besides," Marco said, "the bus probably hasn't come yet, so they'll still be waiting. I promise we'll hurry. Right, Vito?"

"You bet," Vito said casually and not moving any more quickly. "This is the best *mozzarella di bufala* you'll ever taste," he said as he led the boys into a large room filled with vats of water, some steaming, some not, but all a cloudy white with what appeared to be raw pizza dough floating in it.

"Why do you keep calling it that?" Alfie asked, a

bit agitated. Why not just call it mozzarella? And why

couldn't they leave *now*?

"This cheese isn't just plain old mozzarella," Marco explained. "It's not from cow's milk but from buffalo's milk. That's one reason why it's so special, and why it's *mozzarella di bufala*."

Several workers stood before a trough of cloudy water, scooping up white chunks of *mozzarella di bufala,* which they then carefully formed into balls the size of a softball. They then dropped each ball into another trough of water.

"That's the cold water," Marco explained.

Alfie watched with mild interest. Emilia was on his mind, of course, but standing there he realized that the only way he'd ever seen mozzarella was shredded in a bag at the grocery store. He never knew it first swam in water, and he'd never heard of anything being made from buffalo's milk.

"Marco, I've got yours over here," Vito said. He showed them several finished balls of mozzarella. "Finished last night, so this morning they are at perfect freshness."

"Thank you, Vito," Marco said, inspecting each one. "My family can always count on you."

"You'll get your title back this year, we all know you will," Vito said.

Marco stood up a bit straighter and said, "We will, you can be sure."

Marco chose what he decided was the perfect ball of *mozzarella di bufala*, and Vito congratulated him on a strong choice.

"Tell your father I said he better show up to our next game of bocce," Vito said to Marco as Alfie pulled him out the door. "He promised he—"

Alfie and Marco barely heard the rest as they raced back down the hill to find Emilia and Enzo.

# Chapter 8

Alfie found himself in the back of a truck driven by a weathered old man named Sal who worked at the farm and happened to be on his way to town. Marco sat in the back with Alfie, bouncing along as the truck rumbled down the hills and into the city of Naples, coughing up exhaust along the way.

The truck reached the city and began turning through

the winding streets. Alfie was glad to be back where they started and hoped Emilia had somehow found her way back as well. They turned on a street called Via della Sanità, and Marco suddenly called out for the driver to stop. They jerked to a halt.

"What is it? Do you see her?" Alfie said, catching his balance and standing up.

The boys jumped down from the truck. Marco grabbed the basket of ingredients and thanked the driver. "See? Down there," Marco said. The boys shot off down the street.

Alfie saw a sweep of long golden-brown hair and knew it was his sister—and she was with a boy. He called her name as they ran toward them, but she didn't seem to hear. Emilia and Enzo made a turn, and Alfie and Marco followed. The street ended at a building with faded paint and an arched doorway. Enzo led Emilia inside.

As Alfie and Marco raced in behind them, Alfie called out his sister's name again. This time it echoed back a dozen times. He paused and realized there were people here and they were all staring at him.

Emilia walked toward him with a scowl on her face. In a low voice she said, "Alfie! What are you doing?"

Alfie couldn't help himself. He reached out and grabbed his sister in a hug. She was safe. As long as she was okay, he didn't care that she was being ungrateful that he had rescued her.

When he finally gathered his emotions, he said, "I should ask you the same thing. What's going on? What happened?" He looked up. "And where are we?"

He saw frescoes—paintings made right on the ceiling—and tourists milling around and snapping photos as locals kneeled by pews and prayed.

"This is the church of San Gennaro Extra Moenia," Enzo said, stepping toward them casually with his hands behind his back like he was one of the nearby tour guides.

"It is one of Naples's most beautiful churches. It dates back to the 1300s, and the catacombs date back to the second century."

For a moment, Alfie and Marco looked from Enzo to Emilia, trying to understand why they were acting like this was all totally normal.

"You're sightseeing?" Alfie asked, completely dumbfounded.

"Enzi couldn't believe I hadn't seen any of the churches yet," Emilia said. "So he brought me here."

*"Enzi?"* Alfie said. What were they—best friends now?

"It's fine," Enzo said to them. "We were just looking around."

"Get away from my sister," Alfie snapped to Enzo.

"Yes, stay away from my friends," Marco said, setting the basket down to better step between Enzo and the Bertolizzis.

"Now, boys," Emilia said in a mocking tone. Alfie knew she loved this attention, but his only concern was getting her away from this guy.

"Come on, Emilia," Alfie said. "We're going."

"Don't tell me what to do," Emilia said. "I can hang out with whoever I want."

"Trying to act mature for your boyfriend?" Alfie said, knowing it would embarrass his sister. He was frustrated with her.

"This is low," Marco said to Enzo. "Even for you."

"I did nothing wrong," Enzo said, holding up his hands innocently. "It's not my fault if you and your friend care so little about Emilia that you leave her behind on the bus. *That* was low."

"Hey, watch it," Alfie said. He didn't like his loyalty to his sister being questioned.

"Yes, I'm sure *you* were so worried about her well-being," Marco said. "Or maybe more like the well-being of your failing restaurant." Turning to Emilia, he said, "He just wants to spy on us. He knows he's banned from our restaurant. He's just using you."

"I think you're all acting crazy," Emilia said. "All I know is, I was riding a bus with two people and then suddenly I was sitting there all alone. Enzo was the only one there to help me out."

"By bringing you here?" Alfie said.

"He was going to take me to Marco's restaurant," Emilia said. "He figured you'd look for me there."

"Like we'd let him within five blocks of our restaurant," Marco said.

"But when I mentioned I hadn't seen any of Naples," Emilia continued, ignoring Marco, "Enzi very nicely offered to show me around. So don't go acting like you've rescued me or something. I was having a good time until you two showed up."

"And now we're leaving," Alfie said, desperate to take control of the situation. He was also rattled by Emilia's confidence around Enzo, a boy she'd only just met. "Seriously, Emilia. We have to go."

"Fine," she said, as if that was her plan all along. She

turned to Enzo and said, "Thank you, Enzi, for bringing me back to town and showing me this amazing church. I guess I'll see you tonight."

"What happens tonight?" Alfie demanded.

"The pizza festival, obviously," Emilia said with a roll of her eyes. "Why do you think we're gathering all these ingredients?"

"We will not see him tonight," Marco said. "But we have to get going. And this time," he said to Enzo. "You stay here."

Alfie gave Enzo his best scowl and as the three turned to leave, Emilia called out a cheery, *"Ciao!"* to Enzo.

"Couldn't you at least pretend to be on our side?" Alfie said.

"I'm on the side of being a good person," Emilia said. "You know, the kind who doesn't ditch his sister in a strange city."

"As long as he doesn't follow us again," Marco said, holding the basket of ingredients close, "I'll live to see another day."

# Chapter 9

Of course, they hadn't taken more than two steps when Enzo started to follow them again.

"This will never work," Marco said. "We have to lose him."

"He's harmless," Emilia said.

"I can't believe you fell for him," Alfie said, a hint of disgust and disappointment in his voice.

"I didn't fall for him," Emilia quickly said, her face turning a delicate shade of pink. "Whatever. Just don't ditch *me* this time."

"Follow me," Marco said, walking deeper into the church toward the pulpit. "And try and act like you're really enjoying looking around."

"I actually was," Emilia muttered. "Can you believe that people have used this church for over seven hundred years?"

"I guess you learned that from your personal tour guide, huh? Can't you just cooperate? Please?" Why couldn't she just go along with them? It was her fault they were in this situation to begin with.

Alfie and Emilia followed Marco along the sides of the creaky wooden pews, gazing up at the arched columns that led to the heart of the church. The ceiling, covered in ornate gold patterns with brightly colored frescoes, was at least five stories high. It looked more like a museum than a church.

Although the church was quiet, the soft voices of the tourists cast a low rumble. Alfie's sneakers squeaked on the floor, and he tried to walk more delicately to keep them quiet. Enzo lurked farther behind

them, keeping them in his sights. They continued along the black-and-white hexagonal-patterned floor, and Alfie made sure to eye each sculpture that was tucked among the columns, both to look like he was sightseeing and because they were really cool. When they reached the front, they stood to the left of the altar, and Marco turned to look back at the church as if taking it all in. Alfie did the same. An elderly woman spoke to Enzo, her hand resting on his arm. She had no idea what a huge help she was being—she had him cornered.

"This way," Marco said in a low voice, like he was barely moving his lips. "Quickly but quietly."

With Emilia in front of him—he wasn't about to lose her again—Alfie followed Marco through a small side door that they had to duck to get through. They turned a sharp corner to another door that Alfie never would have spotted, since it was adorned with a painting of a saint. The saint's head was ringed with light, and his eyes were looking toward the heavens. Once the three of them stepped through this door and it was shut tight behind them, all sound was completely muffled out and cool air washed over their skin. They carefully stepped down a flight of narrow, crumbling stairs and into a hollow space.

"Where are we?" Emilia whispered, a slight quiver in her voice. Her confidence had vanished.

The three stood side by side, looking out at the cavernous space before them. As ornate as the church was, this was totally bare. All they saw was a low, slightly curved ceiling and long cool tan walls with pockets that looked like open mouths cut out along the sides. The rooms were too dark to see into.

"These are the catacombs of San Gennaro," Marco said as they began to walk the corridors.

"What are catacombs?" Alfie asked.

"Basically old burial grounds," Marco said. "Pretty cool, huh?"

Alfie did think it was cool, but he felt Emilia stiffen beside him. He stepped closer to her and, for a brief moment, squeezed her hand. The way her eyes darted about, he knew she was scared.

Thinking he might distract her, Alfie asked Marco, "I bet these are really old and, like, important to Naples, right?" Emilia's love of history might trump her fear of the catacombs.

"Very important," Marco agreed. "They haven't always just been burial sites. They have also been used as a hospital, a place of study for archbishops, a bomb shelter during war . . . lots of things. Here, I think the door is down this corridor."

As they walked, Alfie noticed that the frescoes were more faded than the vibrant ones upstairs. He ran his hand along the wall—it was cool and rough, and he wondered what hands from the past had also touched it.

Marco stopped abruptly, and Alfie almost slammed into him. Alfie was about to ask what was wrong, but Marco put his finger to his lips. The three stood listening carefully and, off in the distance, Alfie heard footsteps. Emilia grabbed his arm tightly. Her whole body was shivering. He patted her hand as his own heart pounded. He willed away images of ghosts floating through the corridors, angry with anyone who disturbed their eternal peace.

When Marco said, "Someone's coming," Emilia clutched Alfie's arm with new strength. He wanted to reassure her, but as Marco continued to lead them deeper into the dark shadows, he was downright scared as well— of ghosts or of getting caught and thrown in jail, it didn't really matter. All he knew was that they weren't supposed to be there, and now someone or something was coming.

Voices echoed off the walls, and the three friends looked at each other nervously as the sounds got closer and closer. Alfie couldn't even breathe.

"A thousand years?" a voice said. "That's so long!"

Marco let out a long breath. "It's just a tour group," he said. "But let's stay here until they pass."

"A tour group?" Alfie said. He was relieved they weren't going to die or go to jail, but also thought it was really cool that you could tour these things. Officially, anyway.

Once the group passed, Marco, Alfie, and Emilia quickly made their way down another faintly lit corridor where Marco took them up a flight of stairs carved into the wall. After some more quick turns, low ceilings, and tight passageways, Marco threw open one last door and the warmth and crackling energy of the Naples street hit them in the face.

"That ought to take care of him," Marco said triumphantly, and it took Alfie a moment to remember the whole purpose of their trip through the catacombs was to ditch Enzo. There was no way he would find them now. They'd taken so many turns underground that Alfie couldn't even guess where in the city they were.

"Come on," Marco said. "We'll have to run for the tomatoes, just in case he spots us on the street."

As they took off down the street, Alfie noticed how pale Emilia's face had become.

"You okay?" he asked her.

"For now," she said, "I think I'd rather read about the catacombs than go down in them."

Alfie smiled. "They were pretty cool, though, right?"

She cracked a small smile. He knew she was braver than she thought.

# Chapter 10

Marco led them to a tiny shop that almost went unnoticed from the street. There was no sign above the faded blue door, but Marco charged in as if he'd done it a thousand times before. Inside, the cement floors were covered with dust and there were waist-high metal tables throughout. A plump woman greeted Marco.

"Hello, Signora Marta," Marco said back.

"It's about time," Signora Marta said, looking at the clock. "Your father must be getting worried."

"I know." Marco sighed. "We ran into some trouble."

She eyed Alfie and Emilia as if they might be the cause of the trouble Marco had run into.

"Well, come here, come here," Signora Marta said. She lifted a basket filled with the reddest tomatoes Alfie had ever seen.

"Perfect," Marco said as he lifted one to his nose. He breathed in deeply and said, "Ah! They feel and smell perfectly ripe. Friends, you're looking at the best San Marzano tomatoes nature has ever produced!"

"They're really red," Alfie said, peering into the basket. "When I'm old enough to drive, I'm so getting a car that color."

"When I'm old enough to wear lipstick, I'm getting one in that color," Emilia said. She picked up a tomato as well and breathed in its scent. "I've never smelled a tomato that smells so tomatoey."

Marco laughed. "Yes, well, we better get back. Signora's right—Papà is probably having a heart attack right now, wondering where I am."

They said good-bye and rushed back into the streets. Alfie tried to pay attention to the twists and turns, but it was all too confusing. Suddenly, he realized they were back on the street they started on and the zeppole vendor was up ahead. Alfie and Emilia ducked their heads and walked quickly past him on the opposite side of the street. Alfie knew how to get to Trattoria Floreano from here, spotting Pasta Fabbrica on the way.

As excited as Alfie was about the evening's pizza festival, he was becoming quite tired from the day's adventures. Also, the later in the day it got, the more aware he was that he didn't belong here—at least not like this—and he didn't know how they were going to get home. If night came, perhaps Marco would let them crash with him, although Alfie would have to come up with an excuse as to why he and Emilia weren't going back to their parents. Maybe, though, if they fell asleep in Naples, they'd wake up back home. At this point, anything seemed possible.

"There's my boy!" Marco's father said as he walked from the kitchen in long, determined strides. He clapped his hands together and said, "Let's see those beautiful ingredients that will make our family proud."

"Here you are, Papà," Marco said. He handed his father the basket of pizza ingredients.

"And who are your friends, here?" Signore Floreano asked as he began to inspect the ingredients with his eyes, hands, and nose.

"Alfredo and Emilia," Marco said. "They're from America, and I wanted to show them around while their parents—"

"Marco," his father said, stopping him, "is this everything?"

"Yes, Papà, of course," Marco said. "We went to the market, the farm, and the shop."

Signore Floreano looked carefully at his son, and Alfie feared he knew this look. It was kind of like the one his dad gave him when he asked, "Are you *sure* you finished all your homework?" when Alfie knew he hadn't.

"And just how am I supposed to make pizza without mozzarella? Son, how could you?"

Marco's face turned into a mixture of fear and confusion.

"It's in there," Marco said, peering into the basket in his father's hands. "I know it is." But when he looked, it wasn't.

"Distracted by your new friends?" his father said, tossing Alfie and Emilia the sharpest of glances. "And on a day like today, of all days?"

"I did get it, Papà, I swear," Marco said. "It was here."

"Where is it now? Marco, I gave you the most important task. I gave you everything! And this is how you show me you're man enough to start taking on more responsibilities? One day Trattoria Floreano will be yours, but not if you can't be trusted to care for the things we do properly. What do you have to say for yourself?"

"Enzo." That was all Marco had to say. It was clear his father understood perfectly. "He tried to follow us all day long, but I managed to shake him off. And then we sort of ran into him at San Gennaro."

"Just what were you doing there?" Signore Floreano asked.

"It's a long story," Marco said.

"A long story that involved some tour-guiding?" his father said.

Alfie felt terrible. If he hadn't lost Emilia, Enzo never would have found her and taken her to the church, and none of this would have happened. He couldn't let Marco take the blame, especially after all he'd done for him and his sister today.

"Sir," Alfie said, his heart pounding. Signore Floreano's eyes were wide with anger and something else—like he was deciding everyone's fate. "It's my fault this happened."

"No, it's not," Marco was quick to say.

"If it wasn't for me—" Alfie began.

"It's okay," Marco said. "Papà gave me a task, and it was my responsibility to complete it. It's no one's fault but mine."

Alfie then realized that what Marco was doing was the honorable thing—taking responsibility. He was glad he wouldn't personally feel the wrath of Signore Floreano, but he still felt terrible for his role in the outcome of the day. Alfie silently vowed to somehow make it right.

"I'll fix this, Papà, I promise," Marco said.

"There's no time to go back to the farm," Signore Floreano said. "We'll have to go to the market and hope the sellers are still there—and that the mozzarella is up to my standards. But you're not going anywhere. You're finished for the day."

"But Papà—"

"Not another word," Signore Floreano said.

"I can go," Alfie heard himself saying to Signore Floreano. "If Marco needs to stay here and help with the preparations, I can go to the market and get the mozzarella. I want to help."

"Alfie," Emilia said to him. "We'll get lost."

"You're staying here," he said firmly. Turning to

Signore Floreano, he said, "Sir, I know you don't know me or have any reason to trust me, but I do know how important this day and this festival are to you."

"You can't possibly understand," Signore Floreano said, dismissing him.

"But I do," Alfie said. "I spent the whole day listening to Marco talk about how proud he is of the food and what it means to your family. It's all he cares about!" Alfie thought he could see Signore Floreano considering his proposal, so he pressed on. "I'm Italian, too. I know how important family is. Family is everything to us. I would never let my family down, and I promise I won't let yours down."

Signore Floreano looked at him carefully and said, "You don't know the way to the market. And even if you did, you don't know how to choose the mozzarella to my standards."

"I do know the way to the market," Alfie said. "And I watched Marco choose the mozzarella. He told me all about it, so I know what to look for. Signore Floreano, I just want to help your family win your honor back."

Signore Floreano looked between Alfie and Marco. Marco threw his arm around Alfie's shoulder and said, "Please, Papà. Trust my new friends."

Signore Floreano crossed his arms and looked closely at both boys. Finally, he said, "If you're sure, son. If you believe he can do it, then he can go."

The boys relaxed and smiled but Signore Floreano quickly said, "But do not let me down. Understood?"

"Yes," they both said.

"Okay, then," Signore Floreano said. "Off to the market you go. And make sure you choose the *mozzarella di bufala* wisely."

Marco led Alfie to the front of the restaurant, reminding him of the directions to make sure he knew the way.

"Are you sure you don't mind?" Marco asked, relief already flooding his face. "It's just at the market we went to this morning. You remember the stall?"

"Yeah, sure," Alfie said. "I can find the way."

"Alfie," Emilia pressed.

He turned to his sister and said, "It'll be fine. Don't worry, really. It'll be quicker this way."

Lowering her voice so the others couldn't hear, she said, "What if you accidentally go back home without me? I like it here and all, but I don't think I want to be here without you."

Alfie knew the situation was serious, but he also knew they didn't have a clue yet how to fix it. What he could do for now, though, was help the family who had already helped them. So he told her not to worry, got a map from Marco, and set off into the Naples streets alone.

# *Chapter 11*

No way, not in a million years, would Alfie's parents ever let him roam the streets of a foreign city alone. They probably would never let him roam any *American* streets alone, at least not ones they'd only just arrived in. That made this trip to the market ten times more exciting.

Alfie walked the streets with confidence now, easily sidestepping locals as if he were just another Neapolitan rushing out to the market at the end of the day. It was the first time he ever felt truly independent.

Still, he had to pay attention. He looked closely at street signs, paid attention to landmarks like the pasta factory, Pasta Fabbrica, and kept track of north and south, even in the tight, confusing streets. Before he arrived at the Mercato Pignasecca, he spotted someone who had become familiar during this completely unfamiliar day. Leaning against a wall near an alley was a tall, slim boy with unruly, curly hair. Before the boy turned his face toward him, Alfie  knew it was Enzo and his anger instantly rose. When Alfie saw what looked like a softball in his hand, he knew exactly what was going on. Alfie marched through the crowd and straight over to Enzo.

As soon as Enzo spotted Alfie, he pushed off the wall and started to run.

"Hey!" Alfie called, determined not to let him get away. "I see you! Stop!"

He was surprised when Enzo did stop—chasing

someone was never that easy. For a brief moment Alfie was grateful. These streets were Enzo's, and if he'd wanted to lose Alfie in them, he easily could have.

Enzo turned to Alfie and now that he was closer, he saw that he was right. It wasn't a softball in his hand (did Italians even play softball?). It was the cheese—the special *mozzarella di bufala*, to be exact.

"So it's true," Alfie said. "You did it. You stole from Marco."

At least Enzo had the decency to look guilty. He looked down at the cracked sidewalk and ran one hand through his curls. "It's not what you think," he said.

"I don't know what's going on with you and Marco, but stealing is, like, the lowest," Alfie said.

"I wasn't stealing," Enzo said.

"Then how'd this exact ball of mozzarella that we got at the farm get into your hands?" Alfie felt a little like a grown-up demanding answers. It felt kind of good.

"I found it," Enzo said, still not looking Alfie in the

eye—the mark of a true criminal and liar.

"Ha!" Alfie said. "Likely story!"

"I'm telling the truth. I don't lie," Enzo said, finally looking at Alfie. "And I don't steal. The mozzarella fell from Marco's basket in the church. I found it. I was going to return it."

"When? After the pizza festival?"

"Of course not," he said, and Alfie couldn't believe Enzo had the nerve to act offended.

"Why are you being so mean to Marco's family?" Alfie said. "What'd they ever do to you?"

Enzo looked out at the streets. The sun was just beginning to fall behind the mountains above the town. After a moment he said, "Marco's family is *my* family."

"Huh? What do you mean?"

"Marco is my cousin," Enzo said. "I'm also a Floreano. Our fathers are brothers—brothers who hate each other."

*Hate* was such a strong word that Alfie's parents didn't like him to even use it. He had to say he *greatly disliked* tomato soup. So he couldn't imagine using that word to describe how he felt about family. "But why?"

Enzo took a deep breath before he began. "Growing up, our families did everything together, we were always at Trattoria Floreano, and Marco and I were inseparable. Our fathers taught us the family pizza recipe when we were only eight. It's a proud family recipe—one hundred years old! We used to enter the pizza festival together, as one family. Then, three years ago, my father wanted to try a new recipe. He thought he could make the dough even lighter, the sauce a hint sweeter. But Zio Luigi—my uncle Luigi, Marco's father—refused to change the family recipe, which had already won the pizza festival many times and made a success of Trattoria Floreano. My father insisted, and Zio Luigi became so offended that my father would want to break family tradition that he couldn't even look at my papà anymore, much less talk to him or work with him. So Papà decided to start his own restaurant and enter his own pizza recipe. When he actually won the festival last year, Zio Luigi accused him of cheating, and they've been bitter rivals ever since. I'm afraid they'll never speak again."

"Wow," Alfie said. Pizza was clearly serious business if families could be broken up over it. "So you and Marco stopped being friends because of your fathers?"

"Yes," Enzo said. "I guess we felt we had to pick a side, and of course we each chose our own father's. But after talking to your sister this afternoon, on the bus and at the church, I started to realize I didn't want to be a part of it anymore. She talked a lot about you and told me stories of your life in America. Marco was like my brother, and I missed him so much. I *was* following him earlier—my father told me to—and that *is* the mozzarella Marco got from the farm. I was going to return it, honest. After seeing Marco, and seeing how close you and your sister are, I realized that family is more important than a recipe or tradition. Family is the most important tradition of all."

"You both want the same thing—the best pizza in the

world!" Alfie said. "Surely you can make things right. If not with your fathers, then between you and Marco. You don't have to be a part of their fight if you don't want to. Right?"

"That's what I'm hoping," Enzo said. "It's what I was thinking as I stood here, holding the mozzarella. I'm trying to get the courage to go face them. Because if I walk into Trattoria Floreano, I'll be facing the entire family. And it will not be easy."

"We'll do it together," Alfie said. "After all, I guess I owe you one for taking care of my sister and all."

Enzo smiled. "So you admit I wasn't trying to lead her away from you or steal secrets from her?"

"Maybe," Alfie said, although he smiled, too. "So what do you say? Will you come with me to Marco's?"

Enzo fidgeted, putting his hand in his pocket, then taking it out to muss his hair, scratch his arm, and do all sorts of things while looking off down the street. Finally, he looked at Alfie and said, "I guess it can't hurt to try."

## Chapter 12

Alfie knew the way back, but he let Enzo lead. They didn't speak, but Alfie suspected Enzo was nervous by the way he kept bumping into people but didn't seem to notice.

When they walked into Trattoria Floreano, Alfie noticed a new level of preparation was happening behind the counter, with Marco's father working intently and Marco himself nearby at the cutting board. Even Emilia was helping out by rinsing tomatoes. Alfie and Enzo stood for a moment between the restaurant and the kitchen until Alfie nudged Enzo. "Go on," he said. "Say something."

Before Enzo could work up the nerve, Signore Floreano spotted them and called out, "You!" looking directly at Enzo. He turned to his son and asked Marco, "What is he doing here?"

When Marco saw his cousin, he looked confused. As everyone stood in stunned silence, Marco finally asked, "What are you doing here? Haven't you done enough for one day?"

"Marco, please," Enzo said, but any hint of bravery evaporated as every Floreano in the kitchen and restaurant began yelling at him and at each other—and Marco, as if this was his fault.

"His father spits on family tradition," Signore Floreano continued. "They'll stoop to any level to win!"

"How could you?" Marco said to his cousin. "How could you walk into my family's restaurant and try to take from us?" Alfie thought Marco looked more hurt than angry, and he wondered how long it'd been since they'd actually spoken—not yelled—at each other.

"Marco, honestly," Enzo began, "I'm not here to—"

But before he could say more, Signore Floreano

snatched the phone off the wall to call Enzo's father—
Signore Floreano's own brother. "What, now you send
your son to do your dirty work?" he said into the phone,
his face turning redder with each heated moment that
passed.

"Our cheese!" Marco said, pointing to the ball of
mozzarella in Enzo's hand. "I knew it! I knew it, but I still
can't believe it," Marco said, shaking his head and looking
hurt.

"Should I call the police?" a young man hollered from
the restaurant while Signore Floreano yelled into the
phone, gesturing wildly.

Alfie stood watching the whole thing and wondered
if he had made a huge mistake. This was not going well—
not by a long shot. And poor Enzo—Alfie couldn't believe
he was thinking that, but yes, poor Enzo stood there and
took it all. He was getting yelled at from all sides—by the
young man behind him, by his own uncle in the kitchen,
and by his cousin and former best friend, who looked like

he was as disgusted by the sight of him as he would be by the sight of a dead rat in the kitchen.

*"Basta!"* a voice rang through the restaurant. Clapping hands then punctuated each word again: *"Basta! Basta! Basta!"*

The whole place went quiet, and Alfie was shocked to see his own sister standing on top of the counter between the kitchen and restaurant, yelling *enough* to everyone like their mother did when his and Emilia's fighting got out of hand.

Emilia didn't even look surprised or intimidated when everyone turned to her as if awaiting further instructions. She put her hands on her hips and said, "Everyone needs to calm down. If Enzo has walked into this restaurant, it's for a good reason, and I think we should hear him out. This afternoon as we were coming back to town, he said that—"

"You spent time with him?" Signore Floreano said, dropping the phone to the tiled floor and stepping closer to Emilia. "Who are these people you bring into our family business, Marco?"

"Papà, they're my friends," Marco said. "Or I thought they were…"

"We are your friends, but Enzo is family," Emilia continued, refusing to be intimidated. "So I say we hear him out, then you can all decide if you should throw him out on his backside."

Signore Floreano crossed his arms over his puffed belly and with his chin held high, gave a slight nod of agreement. Emilia turned to Enzo and nodded to him as well before stepping down off the counter. Alfie couldn't believe how brave and in control his sister was. Bossy, but in a good way.

Now that all eyes were on him, Enzo seemed more panicked than ever. But Emilia stepped closer to him and said quietly, "It's okay. Just tell them what you told me."

With Emilia by his side, Enzo took a deep breath and began. "This is your cheese, and I was following you."

Another uproar erupted—hands were flying, strong words were uttered, and there were more threats of calling the police—but Enzo pressed on. "I didn't steal your cheese. It fell out of your basket at the church," he said, looking at Marco. "I was following you but not like you think. I followed you because I miss you and I wanted to talk to you. Today used to be our favorite day of the year, better than Christmas. We all spent it together, making and testing and remaking pizza to ensure it was the best in all of Naples. Remember that year we spilled soda into the sauce but didn't tell anyone because we wanted to see how it would turn out? And then everyone tasted it and thought there was something special about it but no one could figure out what?"

A tiny smile appeared on Marco's face. He quickly looked back down to the flour-dusted floor.

"I don't care if our fathers fight, although I wish they wouldn't," Enzo continued. "I just want my friend back. I hope you will forgive me for taking sides with my father."

All of Trattoria Floreano was silent, waiting to hear what Marco would say—or what his father would do. Finally, Marco looked at his cousin and said, "I miss you, too. And I believe you about the mozzarella. You'd never steal, not from anyone for anything. I'm sorry, cousin."

A smile spread on Enzo's face—and on Emilia's and Alfie's as well. Marco and Enzo gave each other a quick hug, and Emilia started clapping and hopping up and down. Alfie noticed Signore Floreano had picked the phone up off the floor and was again speaking into it—speaking, not yelling. As others in the restaurant began applauding for the boys—including the young man who had threatened to call the police—Alfie thought the worst had passed. That is, until the *other* Signore Floreano appeared in the doorway, his eyes bright with an anger similar to his brother's.

*Get ready for round two*, Alfie thought.

# *Chapter 13*

*"Fratello!"*

Enzo's father stood in the doorway of the restaurant. He'd just been on the phone with Marco's father and suddenly, quickly, he was there. Alfie was sure he was angry, but then he slowly spread his arms wide as an equally big smile spread across his face. Soon the brothers, tears flowing down their cheeks, were in their own backslapping embrace, laughing and clapping their hands on their sons' shoulders. Now everyone was smiling and happy and back to work. Except this time, for the first time in years, the entire family would work together on one pizza.

Marco took a break from catching up with his cousin to thank Emilia and Alfie. "If I hadn't met you today, I'd still be without my best friend," he told them. "I'm so glad you chose our restaurant to stop in today."

"I'm glad we did, too," Alfie said, wondering if it was chance or fate that made them walk into Trattoria Floreano out of all the other places on the street. Maybe Zia Donatella had something to do with it? When Alfie looked to his sister, he somehow knew Zia was on her mind as well. "Let's finish helping," Alfie told her. "Then we'll figure out the rest."

She agreed, even though neither knew how this would all end.

Both sides of the Floreano family came to Trattoria Floreano to help make pizza for the festival. After much negotiation—sometimes verging on heated—it was decided that the brothers would use the traditional crust that had been handed down for generations and the updated sauce that began the family feud. Once the pizza was complete, everyone went to the square where judging was taking place. Crowds gathered while music played and people danced, happily celebrating the city's tradition. When the judges came around, all the Floreanos stood, watching the judges' faces to determine how they felt about the new pizza.

They seemed to chew slowly and thoughtfully as every Floreano—and the two Bertolizzis—leaned in and watched carefully and hopefully.

The gentleman who seemed to be the head judge nodded his head slowly and said, "Delicate crust." He took another bite and once again chewed painfully slowly. "Slightly sweet sauce." One more bite, one more excruciating moment of suspense. "Full of flavor." The other judges agreed, and Alfie noticed that the judges had all finished their slices of pizza entirely, instead of only taking a few bites like they did at the other booths. "Your pizza," the judge said to the Floreano elders, "is clearly made with a careful, light touch, melding together the delicate yet explosive flavors of Naples's best ingredients."

Everyone let out a sigh of relief. Now all that was left to do was wait for the winners to be announced. As the judges moved on to the final competitors, Alfie, Emilia, and the Floreanos each had a slice of pizza. Alfie had never tasted pizza so wonderful in all his life. On their first bite, he and Emilia closed their eyes to the heaven that was fresh, made-from-the-heart pizza. Alfie could admit that Presto Pesto didn't come anywhere close to this.

But there was still one thing left—the announcement of the festival winner. The judges all stood on the stage before a microphone as the entire square stopped what they were doing (namely, eating pizza) and listened closely.

"One of the best years we've had at the festival," the judge said. "But the top prize was no contest. This family's pizza showed what Naples is all about—tradition combined with the future of pizza making. Congratulations to . . . Trattoria Floreano!"

The family and Alfie and Emilia cheered and hugged as the brothers playfully teased that it was the change of sauce or the delicacy of the original dough that won them the big prize. Alfie had a different idea. He thought it probably had something to do with the way they felt while making the pizza. They felt happy and relieved now that the family feud was over. Zia Donatella had said herself that how you feel when you cook has a lot to do with how your food tastes, no matter the ingredients.

"For tonight, I insist you and your family stay with us," Marco said to Alfie and Emilia as they walked back to the restaurant. "After all you've done for our family, we must have you as our guests. What time are your parents coming back? Where are you staying tonight?"

Alfie and Emilia eyed each other. The momentum of the day was finally coming to an end, and they had to face reality. How would they get home?

"I wish we could," Alfie said. "But we really have to go meet our parents." At least that wasn't a lie.

Enzo came over to them. "You're not leaving, are you?"

Emilia looked truly sorry. "We have our own family to get back to," she said.

"That's something we can understand," Enzo said.

"We will see you again, though, yes?" Marco asked.

Emilia and Alfie looked at each other. They knew the true answer but couldn't say it out loud. Instead, Alfie said, "I sure hope so."

The entire Floreano family waved good-bye to the Bertolizzi kids, all with promises to see each other again and to please come back anytime. Once they rounded the corner, Alfie could see how sad Emilia was to be leaving. He flung his arm over her shoulder and said, "It'll be okay. And maybe we really will see them again."

"Maybe," she said. "But I guess we have bigger problems right now. As in, how are we going to get home?"

"That," Alfie said, "is the best question I've heard all day."

He had no idea what they were going to do.

# Chapter 14

"Maybe we should go back to the zeppole vendor?" Emilia suggested once they'd turned the corner from Trattoria Floreano, where they'd walked back to in order to get their bearings. "That's where it all started, right?"

"Good idea," Alfie said. He remembered the way, checking street signs and landmarks as he led them through the streets once again. "Maybe we can use the money Signore Floreano gave us for helping out with the pizza to buy another zeppole." Signore Floreano had insisted the Bertolizzis be paid for their help, and Alfie felt better having a little local money in his pocket.

"Only if the vendor guy doesn't chase after us again, that is," Emilia said.

"At least this time we have money. Anyway, maybe he won't recognize us," Alfie said, and he hoped he was right. He really didn't want to end this adventurous day by sitting in some jail cell with no way to call home, much less get home.

It turned out they didn't need to worry about the zeppole vendor. When they got to the street where they'd first arrived, the spot where his cart had been was empty.

"Now what?" Emilia asked.

Alfie didn't have a clue. How do you get back to where you *were* if you have no idea how you got to where you *are*?

"Let's walk and think," Alfie said, hoping inspiration would hit.

Alfie guided them down the streets through Quartieri Spagnoli, past Piazza Martiri and finally the tree-filled lawns of Villa Comunale where they faced the Gulf of

Naples. Maybe they should catch a boat somewhere—but where? Maybe, in reality, his parents really were here, in Naples? Or this was some sort of bizarre dream? He didn't believe that, even as he didn't know *what* to believe. He only knew today felt as real as any day he'd had back home. As much as he didn't want it to end, he knew he wanted to be in his home, with his family. So they'd have to keep thinking.

They spotted a lone vendor on the lawn of Villa Comunale, selling to couples and late-day stragglers hoping to catch the sun setting into the sea. The smell of fresh fish and something fried from the vendor sent his stomach rumbling despite the excellent pizza they'd had not long ago.

"Want to get a snack?" he asked his sister.

"Sure."

They went to the vendor, a smiling old man with brown eyes that sparkled in the fading sun, who sold fried-fish sandwiches wrapped in white paper.

"Squeeze of lemon?" the vendor asked, holding up a
lemon wedge.

Alfie shrugged and said yes, and the vendor squeezed a little lemon juice over the sandwiches. "Let's sit close to the water, on that wall over there," Alfie suggested after they'd paid for their sandwiches. He led his sister carefully across Via Francesco Caracciolo and up onto the wall. They let their feet dangle over the edge of the wall. The cool, salty air blew across their faces as they bit into their fried-fish sandwiches.

"Oh my gosh," Alfie said, looking down at his food.

"I know," Emilia said. "This is so good."

It was—crispy crust holding in the flaky whitefish with a hint of zest from the lemon. And the homemade bread made it even more delicious.

"You remember that time," Alfie began, "we went to the beach and you were so scared to get in the water that Mom had to bring you a bucketful and let you dip your toe in so you'd know there was nothing to be afraid of?"

"I wasn't afraid," Emilia said indignantly. "I'd heard some other kids saying there might be jellyfish and I just didn't want to get stung."

"Oh yeah. You made Dad promise you that there weren't any jellyfish before you'd go in."

"He said it was a jellyfish-free beach and it was illegal for them to swim there," she said, smiling.

"And later that day it was Dad who got stung," Alfie said, and they both laughed.

"He kept hopping around the beach, holding his leg out to strangers, going, 'It's a sting, what should I do?'"

"Mom was so embarrassed."

"*I* was so embarrassed," Emilia said.

"That was the trip I learned to bodysurf," Alfie said, looking out at the water. *Do kids here in Italy bodysurf?*

he wondered. He took another bite into his sandwich, remembering how it felt to coast on the waves.

"That was the trip I totally beat you at Frisbee."

"You can't win at a game where no one keeps score," Alfie said.

Emilia took another bite and said, "There was that little shack on the beach that sold Cokes in glass bottles that you had to return for a refund. And the fish and chips."

"Those fish and chips," Alfie said, "were the *best*."

"Best ever," Emilia agreed.

They sat quietly on the wall and remembered that trip and how the fish and chips tasted crispy and salty and so yummy after a long day in the sun and how much they'd laughed and played. Alfie remembered how Mom leaned back into Dad as they watched him and Emilia stuff their faces with the shack food. "What beach bums," Dad had said.

Alfie didn't realize he'd closed his eyes at the memory until something strange began to happen—strange but familiar. A shift in the air. For a moment he felt he couldn't even open his eyes, but even so, everything around him felt different, even smelled different. When he finally opened his eyes, everything had changed. It wasn't the Gulf of Naples he saw now. It was his great-aunt Donatella, smiling at him and his sister in the kitchen of their own home. It had happened. Again. Except now they were home.

"Zia Donatella?" Alfie said, not quite believing all that had happened.

"Well," she said with a wink. "What do you think?"

# Chapter 15

"You have to stop telling people," Emilia said to her brother on their walk home from school the next day. "No one believes us."

"How could I not tell people I spent the day in Naples, Italy, yesterday?" Alfie said, surprised his sister would pass up an opportunity to tell the entire school about their travels and adventures. "Don't you want to tell your little friends about Enzo?"

"Be quiet," she said, slugging him in the arm.

Alfie pretended like she socked him hard.

"How do you think we can get back?" he asked. He wanted to see Marco again, taste more food, and explore more twisting streets.

"We're still not sure how we got there in the first place," Emilia said. "I'm not even sure it all really happened."

"You know it did," Alfie said as they walked up to their front door. "And I know you want to go back just as much as I do."

"Maybe. I just wonder—what's that noise?" Emilia asked as they shut the front door behind them. "Is that . . . Mom and Zia? In the kitchen?"

"No way," Alfie said.

In the kitchen they found their mom laughing as she sliced vegetables. Next to her, Zia Donatella shredded cheese on a box grater. "Always with the grating!" she said in mock anger.

"I could go buy the pregrated kind," Mom said. She wiped the tears from her eyes.

"Pregrated!" was all Zia Donatella could say to that, which made Mom laugh even harder.

"What's going on?" Alfie asked.

"Oh, hi, kids," Mom said. "Nothing. Just dinner." She tossed the vegetables she'd been slicing into a pan of hot oil. It crackled and sizzled and she gave it all a quick stir.

"You're making dinner?" Emilia asked. "As in, cooking it?"

"Don't tease your mother," Zia Donatella said. "She's actually a very good cook."

"But she never cooks," Alfie said. She was always too busy with work, just like Dad.

"Hush, you kids!" Mom said. "You're making me look bad in front of Zia. Oh, you can stop grating the cheese."

"*Mama mia!* My arm is about to fall off!" Zia said, and they both fell into another fit of laughter.

Dad came into the kitchen and looked as confused by the scene as Alfie and Emilia did.

"They're cooking," Alfie deadpanned.

"Dinner?" Dad asked.

This time everyone laughed—what else would they be cooking?

Mom and Zia made a feast of pasta with fresh vegetables for dinner, and everyone got to help. Emilia turned the regular butter into herb butter, and Alfie sliced the warm *ciabatta* bread fresh out of the oven. Dad made the salad with ingredients Zia Donatella set out for him.

They all sat around the table together and dug into the meal, which was hot and fresh and tasted better than any meal they'd had together at home. Having Zia Donatella there was like the freshly made whipped cream on top of the gelato they'd be having for dessert—something to make the night extraspecial.

But as closely as they looked, Zia Donatella gave no hint of what had happened to Alfie and Emilia, if she knew about it or had anything to do with it. Even when prompted with questions like, "Zia, does this food remind of you Naples? Of, like, going to Naples and walking around the cobblestoned streets?"

"Yeah, Zia," Alfie said. "Like walking along Via Vecchia and going to the *mercato*?"

"Alfie, you've been staring at those maps too much," Dad said. "He's got the streets memorized and everything!"

Alfie thought he saw Zia's eyebrow shoot up in acknowledgment, but it was so quick he couldn't be sure.

After dessert, Alfie said, "Mom, don't forget our school potluck tomorrow. We signed up for pizza, so we need to order it in the morning." Alfie was actually sort of curious to eat delivery pizza now that he'd had the freshest of handmade pizzas in Naples. Would he still love Presto Pesto?

"Order?" Mom said. "We're not ordering anything. We're making it!"

"Do we have tomatoes, fresh mozzarella, and basil?" Alfie asked.

"Since when do you know about making pizza from

scratch?" Mom said, getting up from the table. From the pantry she took out a bowl with a cloth towel draped over the top. She pulled it back gently to give Alfie and Emilia a peek, but they could smell it before they saw the fresh, rising dough. What smelled better than that? Mom put it back and said, "Zia and I will make it in the morning and bring it fresh to your school. No need to worry."

"Zia's going to help make it?" Emilia asked, and Alfie could see that something good was whisking through her mind.

"Yes, of course," Mom said.

"Pizza is my specialty," Zia said.

"It's really amazing," Mom said. "Simple, but full of flavor."

"As long as the tomatoes are from the hills of Mount Vesuvius," Emilia said.

"Very good, young lady," Zia Donatella said.

Mom looked at Emilia and said, "How do you know that?"

"You know, history lessons at school and stuff,"

Emilia said, as if it were no big deal. "We learned about the volcano, and our teacher told us other stuff about the hills surrounding Naples."

"Maybe our kids really are Italian," Dad joked.

"Sometimes I feel like I barely remember Naples, even though I grew up there," Mom said.

"Same here," Dad said. "I have little flashes of memories, like of the old pasta factory and the wall down by the gulf, but not much else."

Alfie thought he would burst at the mention of things he himself had just seen and experienced, but Zia Donatella gave him a look that said he should play it cool. So as hard as it was, he did his best. "We should all go together," he said. "Visit Italy, hang out in Naples. You could show us where you grew up."

"And where you used to get pizza," Emilia said. Alfie was positive that she was thinking of Trattoria Floreano. What if their parents had eaten there as children? They might know the Floreano brothers!

Mom looked at Dad across the table and said, "You know, we should really think about doing that."

Dad smiled back and said, "No reason why we shouldn't."

Alfie and Emilia happily finished their gelato knowing that something magical had happened that evening—something that had everything to do with food, Zia Donatella, and the simple act of eating together.

# Chapter 16

When Mom dropped off the still-hot pizzas at school the next day, Alfie had one very important question to ask her.

"Zia helped make these, right?"

"I can cook on my own, you know," Mom said. "But yes, she did help. I kept her on cheese duty." She ruffled his hair and told him to have a fun lunch with his friends. The school had combined grade levels for the potluck, and Emilia and her friends were in his group as well.

The classroom was transformed into a mini United Nations, with flags from all over the world hung on the walls, and tables lined up around half the room filled with foods as colorful as the flags themselves. Ms. Esch and Ms. James, two of the teachers helping out today, worked on setting up the dishes and making sure there were plenty of plates, napkins, forks, and even chopsticks for all the students.

"Hey, Alfredo," called a boy in Alfie's class who was sort of his friend but also sort of annoying. His name was Charlie and he was pointing to the pizzas that Alfie was keeping a careful watch on. Alfie felt protective of them, but he wasn't yet sure why. "Did you fly this in from Rome?"

Charlie was trying to tease Alfie, but Alfie wouldn't let him. "You mean Naples, and no, my mom and aunt made it fresh."

"Yeah, sure," Charlie said. "So, what—you're going to Rome tomorrow or something?"

"Not sure," Alfie said, shrugging like he was actually considering it.

"Hey, Alfie," said Becky, a girl in his class who leaned

over the box of pizza. "When, exactly, did you go to Italy?"

"Not long ago," Alfie said. The way Becky leaned over the pizza made him think that she actually wanted to hear about his trip—unlike Charlie. "If you want I could tell you all about it after school. Like how I escaped from a thief through an underground cemetery."

"Wow! Really?" Becky said.

"Really," Alfie said.

"Excuse me, Alfredo?" Emilia said. She eyed Becky. "A word, please?"

"I'll be right back," he told Becky.

Emilia literally pulled him by his arm across the room to a corner by the bratwurst of Germany. "Hey, listen," she said, speaking quietly. "I was thinking. Did Mom say Zia Donatella helped with the pizzas?"

"After she got totally offended at me for asking, she said she did."

"So you know what this means," Emilia said. "When people start biting into our pizzas, it's gonna be *wham-o*!

Transported back to Naples!"

"I know!" Alfie said. "I was thinking the same thing!" Alfie pictured himself acting as tour guide through the city, showing his classmates how to get to the market, Trattoria Floreano, the catacombs, and more. Maybe this time they'd have time to visit Mount Vesuvius. Alfie knew his sister would love seeing it.

"Okay, everyone!" Ms. Esch called to the students. "Time to present our dishes."

The students gathered in the center of the room. Students were in teams of two or three to present their country or region and the food they brought to represent it. They listened through bangers and mash from England, tamales from Mexico, couscous from Morocco, and lots more. When it was time for Alfie and Emilia to present, Emilia took the lead.

"Our family is from Italy," she said proudly. "My mom and dad moved here when they were about our age."

"Not together, though," Alfie said, and the teachers

laughed and so did some of the students. "They met when they were in college and already living here."

"Well, yeah, of course," Emilia said. "This pizza is like the pizza from the city of Naples, in southern Italy. What makes this pizza special to the people of Naples is that it doesn't have many ingredients but the ingredients it does have are really good and fresh and delicious."

"Also, it's made from scratch by my mom and great-aunt, who both grew up in Naples," Alfie added.

"So, enjoy!" Emilia said, throwing her arms wide.

Finally all the presentations were done and it was time to sample the food. Students could choose to eat from whichever country they wanted to taste, and Alfie and Emilia watched closely as some of their classmates gathered around their pizza. The siblings already had their slices, ready to bite into them as soon as their friends and the other students began eating.

"Here, Becky. I saved you a slice," Alfie said, handing Becky a plate with a big slice on it. Emilia rolled her eyes, but Alfie pretended not to see.

Becky took a bite of the pizza. "Mmmm! It's really good!" she said through a mouthful.

"Doesn't it just taste like Naples?" Alfie said.

"Sure, I guess," she said. "Have you ever had the Taco Explosion pizza at Presto Pesto? It's amazing!"

Alfie couldn't believe it, but he actually had to turn away from Becky at that comment.

He stood with Emilia and they watched as Daniel McKenzie picked up a slice and tipped the end into his mouth. He chewed and talked to his friend Austin, and soon Austin picked up a slice as well. But nothing happened. Three and four and five and more students ate the pizza but nothing was happening—no one was going anywhere.

"Why aren't they being transported?" Emilia asked.

"Maybe we have to eat at the same time," Alfie said.

"And tell stories of Naples," Emilia said. "Remember, Zia told us about her home as we ate the zeppole."

They went to the center of the crowd and worked it as best they could.

"In Naples the streets are really narrow and made of cobblestones," Emilia said as she chewed a bite. "You have to be careful where you walk, or you'll trip on the stones or bump right into someone walking really fast by you."

"Everyone is in a rush, but it's because they all have something important to do," Alfie added, trying to think quickly. "It's a busy city with lots of small cars rushing through the streets."

"Yeah, can't you just see it?" Emilia asked.

"The crowds? The people?" Alfie said. "The streets?"

"And the tiny cars?" Charlie said. "Yeah, we got it, dude."

Soon the pizza had been devoured and everyone had moved on to gyros from Greece.

"Why didn't it work? What'd we do wrong?" Emilia

asked. "Maybe we somehow dreamed it after all."

"I don't believe that," Alfie said. "And I don't think you do, either."

"Maybe Zia has to be here?" Emilia said.

"Right after school, let's go straight home," Alfie said. "We'll ask Zia to make us something—maybe more zeppole. Don't say a word about Naples or Italy or travel or anything. Just tell her we love her cooking . . ."

"And her stories," Emilia added.

"And we'll see what happens. Deal?"

"Deal!" Emilia said.

They could hardly wait until the final bell of the day. When they were dismissed, Alfie and Emilia raced out the front doors and down the sidewalk toward home. They hopped up and down at the crosswalks waiting for the light to change, and when they finally made it up the front walk to their house, Alfie practically broke the front door, he slammed through it with such force. But inside, the house was quiet.

"Zia Donatella?" Alfie called, and Emilia followed him into the kitchen.

"*Ciao, ragazzi!* There you beauties are!" Zia Donatella said from behind the kitchen island. The counter in front of her was covered with bowls, pots, spice jars, and all kinds of fresh ingredients. "So, are you ready for the next adventure . . . ?"

# A Note from Giada

Pizza is the first thing I remember cooking. I would make Neapolitan pizza with my grandfather, and as we cooked he would tell me of his adventures in the beautiful city of Naples. It made me dream of adventures of my own, and it made the pizza we made together taste even more delicious!

My grandfather was born in Torre Annunziata, a city in the province of Naples, and as we kneaded dough, sliced tomatoes, and grated cheese together, he would tell me about the sights and smells of Naples. And when I first visited Naples, I understood why my grandfather loved the city so much.

Naples is one of the oldest cities in Europe, and its architecture ranges from medieval castles and ancient ruins to beautiful churches and stunning piazzas. And the food of Naples reflects that it has been a crossroads for world travelers throughout its long history.

Even though those days of making pizza with my grandfather are gone, and I'm now making pizza with my daughter, his memories of Naples will stay with me forever.

Xo